Jehanne

John Gumbs

Published by John Gumbs
Publishing partner: Paragon Publishing, Rothersthorpe
First published 2018
© John Gumbs 2018, London

ISBN 978-1-78222-571-3

Book design, layout and production management by Into Print
www.intoprint.net
+44 (0)1604 832149

To
Heidi Koren, for encouraging me to write Jehanne. When I was in a negative mood, she kept telling me that I could do it.

I would also like to acknowledge all those who have written about Jehanne. And all those who have written the history of Great Britain and France.

1.

At Domremy

Domremy first came on the scene around 1070 AD. It is a small village connected with many bosses. It came under the authority of Vaucouleurs; and so was part of the kingdom of France. It is located in the township of Coussey of the district of Neufchateau. Now when we get to where Jehanne lived, we called this the Southern part, belonging to the Barrois area. Greux is only 0.87km away.

∼

My name is Jean Gretier and I live in the village of Domremy. I was born in the same year as Jehanne on the 31st March 1412. My parents were farmers just like the family of Jehanne. In the village, she was known as Jeannette, but when she later left and went into France, she called herself *Jehanne La Pucelle* (the little maid). Her father was Jacques d'Arc and he was one of the leaders of the village. A well-built man, good features, solid long nose; and a pleasant face. His wife Isabel Romee was a very deeply religious woman. She had made many pilgrimages. She was a good-looking woman, kindly and sympathetic. Both Jacques and she had five children – three boys and two girls. Their names were: Jacquemin, Pierre, Jean, Catherine and Jeannette. They lived in a cottage connected to that of Mengette's. Mengette was a close friend of Jehanne. The cottage had a shed-styled roof; it was not far from the church which was located next door, on the road that led to Greux.

At the back of the cottage was a fair sized garden, close to the cemetery. On this day, aged 10, I stood outside Jeannette's house with a few other boys and girls, waiting for her to come out so that we could go and play like we normally did on certain days. The river Meuse was about one hundred metres away flowing on its northward journey. There was a big tall tree just in front of the main door; and at the side there were crawling plants making their way across the wall, and up to the top of the shed roof. Around the house were many beautiful trees and plants. Jeannette finally came out in her patched red dress; and greeted all who had been waiting for her. There was Hauviette and Mengette, her two best friends. Hauviette was very close to her, slept at her house many times. There was also Colin, along with Jean Waterin, and a few others. Inside the door Isabel was saying "hello" with a big smile on her face. Normally, the girls always get together and go for walks and visiting shrines, while the boys go off to the woods and play soldiers and see if we could see any dragons. It was told to us that there were dragons in those woods in ancient times. Up to this day we had not seen any. Today, the boys and girls stayed together. We all went up to the beech tree. It was known as the *Fairies' tree*. It was a few hours from noon and we knew that we had to be back for lunch. Sometimes Jeannette and I would break sticks and pretend that they were swords or lances – we were the soldiers handling them. Jeannette was very good and many times she broke through and touched me with her stick; all the other children would clap and cheer. Sometimes we would play and dance around the beech; and then go and drink from the spring that was nearby.

"Jeannette," I said, "you are very good, if you keep practising, when you get older, you can go and fight for the Dauphin."

"Yes," Jeannette said. "I'd like to be a knight on horseback and chasing those Godons back to where they came from. I'd also like to be the one responsible for making the Dauphin a proper king."

Hauviette said, "Jeannette, you're a real lover of France, but only men are the ones fighting for the country."

"Women are fighting as well," Jeannette told her. "They're not dressed in armour as the men are; but they are fighting in other ways. I will be dressed in armour just like a knight."

Colin said, "Stop dreaming, Jeannette. You will get married and settle down with children."

"*Oh! No,* Colin! I am not going to get married."

Jean Waterin broke in. "How do you know?"

Jeannette turned to him and said: "I just have the feeling. I don't want to get married."

I said to Jeannette, "By the way, the king is a proper king. He was crowned at Poitiers the same year his father died."

"He becomes a proper king," Jeannette said, "when he is anointed with the sacred oil in Riems; just like all the ancient kings before him."

"That's going to be hard," I muttered, "seeing that the enemy has control over all that area."

"When I"m leading the troops, it shall be much easier to get through those areas ruled by the Burgundians and by the English."

The rest of the children started laughing. Mengette said, "*You,* Jeannette, leading the Dauphin's troops? Be serious. Such a thing is not possible."

"I tell you Mengette, you will hear about it. This day you can laugh, because I'm still young; but it will definitely come to pass."

I said: "It would be very hard for a woman to do that sort of work."

"Why?" Jeannette asked. "Are they only good for sewing and spinning, and household work?"

"Some women," I told Jeannette, "are capable of more than that: but have you ever heard of a woman leading lords, knights, squires and noblemen into battle?"

"You will hear of it one day, I tell you, Jean. You'll definitely see it with your own eyes."

As we walked along I asked Jeannette, "Do you believe in fairies?"

She answered. "I heard my godparent talked about them but I haven't seen them with my own eyes."

"Ah! They're those little men and women roaming about in areas around the Fairies' Tree, and can only be seen by certain people. Wait a minute... Do you see that?"

"What?" Jeannette looked at me while I looked in the direction of the green plant.

"Do you know," I turned to her and said, "that if you have one of those plants in your possession, that you can become very rich?"

"That's a long tale," Jeannette replied.

"It's a magical plant," I told her. I will pull it up and you will see that it's shaped like a man or a woman at its roots. But here is what I want you to do. Cover your ears so that you do not hear it when it screams."

"What do you mean? The plant will cry out? How's that possible?"

"Because it is magic. Do you believe in magic? Well, put your hands over your ears. I will pull it up and let you see."

The other children were nearby and heard what I had said. Jeannette, with both hands covering her ears, waited to see what would happen. The other children covered up their ears also. They eagerly watched as I moved towards the plant. I grabbed it just below its leaves and gave it a jank. A strange sort of screeching noise came from it. With the plant in my hand, I turned to Jeannette and the other children, "You can take your hands away now, it's ok!"

Colin asked, "Why didn't you cover up your ears like we did?"

"I wasn't afraid, that's why. Even though I heard the story said that if you hear the scream it can drive one crazy."

They all began to look at the plant more closely. Jeannette said, "It truly looks like a human being. What are you going to do with it?"

"I will take it back and keep it with me."

We played around some more, picking flowers for our parents. It was now getting close to lunch time. We got back just in time to see Jeannette's father and brothers coming in from the fields. Her sister Catherine was home and helping her mother. Jeannette's family always invited me to come and eat with them. We sat at the big solid table with stools around it: and on the left hand side was the fireplace with wood burning furiously. When we were all seated, Isabelle and Catherine brought the soup and the bread, and we started the lunch meal. Jeannette told her father about the mandrake. He said that it was just old tales told; and that there was nothing in it. We talked about other things to do with farming, of Vaucouleurs and Maxey where the Burgundian village was. Then we got unto the Dauphin. Jacques told us quite a lot about what had taken place so far between the English, the Burgundians and the French. He said that France was in a dreadful state, and that it needed a miracle to save it. I mentioned to him that we got some history lessons in our school and that I had taken interest in them.

"What are you going to do later?" he asked.

I told him that when I reached the age of 12 that I would try to be a page, then work my way up, and eventually become a knight or a lord. Jacques said that he was not able to go and fight because someone had to stay and make sure that the people had food from the farms. Pierre and Jean, Jeannette's brothers, said that they would like to go and fight for France and the Dauphin. After lunch, I said so long, and went down to my parents. Everyday afterwards I saw Jeannette. We continued with our dance and singing, and walking through the fields and meadows, rolling down the hills that were just above us. There was also a wood that was known as the *Bois Chesnu*. It was full of oaks and other trees – thick as ever. When we danced, the boys would hold the girl's right hand up in the air, and with the right hand on the hip, we dance forward, then a jig to the right, then to the left, then a turn-around, with all the others following in a half-circle. The girl is always on the left. You could see on the faces of the parents who were watching that they enjoyed it; then they would all clap their hands. Later on, Jeannette didn't dance as much as she used to do. She was more often in the church than ever. I approached her one day and said to her, "Jeannette, is there something wrong? The reason why I asked is because I see that you don't take part in the dances any more, you just stand and watch."

She said that there was nothing wrong and that she liked to go to church. I knew that she had gone many times with her sister Catherine and some of the other girls to the chapel of Bermont, just up on the hill. I said to her, "We miss you taking part, for you are one of us, and you can sing well."

Jeannette said: "In the beginning I took part, but now I must ease off a bit, I will come now and then, but for now I'm very busy with the affairs of the church."

"Yes, I can see that!"

Jeannette asked, "Don't you like the church?"

I said: "The church is okay for the community, but it should not take up all our time. I like to be around my friends playing games, playing at being soldiers; and make believe that we are on horses; dressed in armour; and going into battle. Just like when we go down against the other boys at Maxey. You have seen many times how we came back, sometimes with our clothes torn, and with bloody faces."

Jeannette said: "You came back with the victory. It wasn't nice to see the blood, but the feeling was good to know that you won. Maxey is part of Burgundian territory, but I am from Domremy."

We talked some more and then parted.

2.

Tours

Jehanne has found herself in Tours where she met up again with her childhood friend, Jean Gretier. His parents owns a guest house and Jehanne is staying there with her group. She tells Jean Gretier all that took place since he left Domremy.

Two years later, my family left Domremy and went all the way to Tours. It was sad to leave all my friends behind, and Domremy as well. Such a beautiful peaceful place with all the beautiful country side with all the different colors; and in winter, all the whiteness. Still, that was the way of life, and I had to go where my parents went.

In Tours, they ran a four-storey guest house, with a big courtyard in the front. I worked at the convent and helped my parents with the guest house. I didn't see Jeannette again until she turned up at our guest house with a small group. I was already seventeen – and so was Jeannette. Messengers had arrived a week before she came to let us know about accomodating her and her group. I had heard rumours about a Maid who had left the Marshes and was on her way to see the Dauphin at Chinon.

I hadn't the faintest idea that it was Jeannette who was the Maid. She came with her little group around the first week of April 1429. As she rode into the courtyard on her black charger, I greeted her, half shouting, "Jeannette!"

She replied, "Jean! how good to see you again, my friend. By the way, I am not called Jeannette any more. I call myself Jehanne, the Maid. Beside me, on either side are my two brothers, Pierre and Jean, you already know them. And there is my Squire and bodyguard, Jean D'Aulon. My two pages, Louis and Raymond, and my two heralds, Guyenne and Ambeville. Father Pasquerel is my personal confessor. This is a very big place you have here. Is it doing well?"

"Yes, we get along fine running it." I went round and shook the hand of each one in her group. When they all had dismounted, I escorted them inside, while their horses were taken care of I introduced them to my parents, my wife and my young child, just a year old. Pierre and Jean and Louis already knew my parents. Louis wasn't born in Domremy but in Neufchateau. Pierre, I was told was born in 1408; Jacquemin in 1402; and Jean in 1409.

After Jehanne and her group had settled in they came down to the dining area where there was a very long table with chairs around it. The fireplace was on the right with logs of wood burning away. When we were all seated and had something to drink, Jehanne started relating her story to me of how she came to be where she was now. She dipped a piece of bread in her drink, which was wine, and placed it in her mouth. She said to me: "A year after you left Domremy, in the month of May, I was in my father's garden, with the cemetery next to it, and the church on the other side, when suddenly I heard this beautiful soft voice; and at the same time, a light very bright, appeared on the right of me. I shuddered and became afraid, but the voice console me and told me that I must be a good girl, and that I must keep on going to church. It told me that I would raise the siege of Orléans; and that I must go into France."

"Did you know who was talking to you?" I asked her. "Did

you get a name? My God Jehanne, you have been chosen to save France."

Jean d'Arc said: "That's why we are here to give backing to our sister. We believe in her. We believe that she can do the things that she said that she would do."

Pierre d'Arc said: "Yes, she gets our support."

"Go on Jehanne, tell me more."

"Well," Jehanne said, "I had to go around with this secret for almost five years. I couldn't let any one know about it."

"You didn't even tell your parents? What about the Cure? Didn't you say something to him? And your best friend Hauviette?"

"No. I kept it all to myself. It was too dangerous to let the Burgundians know about it. The voice told me to go and see the governor at Vaucouleurs. Now I had to make a plan to get away from my parents without them suspecting anything."

"I know," I said, "if I were around at the time, you would have told me, and I would have tried my best to help you."

"I know Jean, that you would have helped me. I got my uncle to come and fetch me. I would be nurse to his wife who was having a baby. He came and we walked along the road, saying goodbye to only a few. I could not say goodbye to Hauviette, for I knew how much it meant to her to be around me; and I knew that it would hurt her a lot, so I just went away without telling her. I did say goodbye to Mengette."

"I know your uncle, I met him a few times, he's a nice fellow."

"He's kind, and I knew that I could trust him. He didn't let me down."

"He lives in Burey-Le-Petit, not far from Domremy."

Jehanne said that his wife's name was Jeanne. I don't think that I have met her. Jehanne told me about when she was 12 that she went to Neufchateau to help a woman there whose name was La Rosse. She mentioned that in 1428 there came some raiders and robbers pillaging and burning houses in Domremy. The church was half burnt so that the people had to go to Greux for their services. I was aghast to hear such horrible news after I had left. Jehanne continued: "I stayed a few weeks with my uncle, then I went and lived with Henry le Royer and his wife Catherine. My uncle took me for the first time to see Robert de Baudricourt – the governor. He didn't take me serious enough to send me to the Dauphin. He told my uncle to take me back and box my ears. I forgot to tell you that I had this man who took me to court saying that I had promised to marry him."

"Was he mad or what? You getting married? I had the feeling that you would not have settled down to married life. Having seen you going to church so often and praying, I said to myself, 'no, this one is not that type.'"

Jehanne carried on, "I had to go to Toul to defend myself. The voices had already told me that I would win the case; and I did. I had also to go and see the Duke of Lorraine. He thought that I was some sort of healer who could heal his sickness, but he was wrong. While I was there I asked him to let his son escort me to the Dauphin. He just gave me a black horse and four francs."

"You mean his son Rene d'Anjou? The Duke had five sons by Allison Dumay."

"Yes, the young nobleman."

"I'm getting the feeling Jehanne," I said to her, "that you were in quite a hurry to try and get to the Dauphin."

"I had to be with the Dauphin before Lent. I even had my uncle and a few other old men to escort me, but after a while, I told them to take me back to Vaucouleurs. It wasn't a good idea to try and make such a long journey with those old men."

Pierre d'Arc said: "Papa and mama were worried over you

especially when they did not get any news about you from Vaucouleurs. Papa had a dream that you were planning to run away with soldiers; he didn't want that to happen, and he said that if he hadn't drown you, that we, your two brothers must do so. But we saw and believe something more than what papa saw or believed. That's why we are here with you."

Jehanne said: "Thanks Jean and Pierre for believing in me. You know that I will never lie to both of you. I just have to do what I am told to do, no matter what happens."

Jean d'Arc said: "We always knew that there was something special about you. Mama really taught you well. And you're so good at sewing and spinning. You would have made a good wife for some nobleman."

Father Pasquerel was quiet for a long time, he didn't say much. He said, "Jehanne is a good pious girl, very courageous, simple and devout. I believe in her that is why I shall follow her wherever she goes. By the way, Saint Michael who came in a vision to Jehanne is patron Saint of France along with Saint Remy."

I asked Jehanne, "Did Saint Remy appear to you?"

"No," she answered. Saint Michael told me that Saint Catherine and Saint Margaret will both come to give me council."

Father Pasquerel said: "Saint Catherine of Alexandria was a virgin and a great martyr. She is known as Catherine of the wheel. She received a vision: and when she was 18 she consulted with over fifty philosophers. Many of them converted to the Christian faith along with many soldiers. Saint Margaret too, was a virgin known as Saint Maria the grand martyr, daughter of a pagan priest. Her mother died in child birth. She was nursed by a very religious woman. Margaret took on the Christian faith and consecrated her virginity to God."

Jehanne said: "That is exactly what I did from the moment Saint Michael appeared to me. I decided there and then not to get married, and to stay a virgin as long as God wants it to be so. My parents tried to marry me off, but I refused; and that's why I ended up in Toul in the courthouse."

My wife said: "Well, your two women saints were virgins and martyrs, and you yourself are a virgin. You probably end up as a martyr too."

Jehanne replied, "I don't know what I'll end up as, but I do know that there are two things my voices told me that I will do; and that is to raise the siege of Orléans; and to crown the Dauphin at Riems."

I said, "From what I know, Jehanne is a very pious young girl, very devoted to God and the Saints. She believe that she will achieve what she sets out to do. Her mother was the only one who taught her about the faith. She is very close to her family. She loves them very much even though she didn't get on well with her father. He was very strict. He didn't want her to be running around with soldiers like the camp women do. All what he wanted was for her to be married, and to settle down and have her own family." I paused, then carried on. "France is in a bad state at the moment, and with all the battles they've already lost to the English, this one at Orléans calls for good leadership and endurance. The English has proven many times over that they're a very powerful force to deal with. When Henry V invaded France, he came over with about 12,000 men He had laid siege to the port of Harfleur. The French fought like mad; the siege took longer than had expected; the town later surrendered. The king then decided to march his army across the French countryside to Calais. His own council thought that it was a crazy idea, and they warned him against doing so. On the 25th October 1415, the English came to a village called

Agincourt. All this time, a French army was tracking them, and finally intercepted them. The English were really outnumbered, tired, and half hungry. The English king led his army into battle giving the French a heavy blow. They fought in a thin strip of muddy land, which had been soaked with rain from the night before. The French in their plate armour got bogged down, and were not able to fight properly.

Henry was there encouraging his troops and fighting hand to hand. I think that that battle was a battle the French will never forget. Many great nobles fell, and were taken for prisoners and for ransom."

Jehanne said: "I know that I shall be victorious at Orléans, I'm not afraid, for I know that God shall be with me, and the English shall be driven away from Orléans and finally from France."

"I will join you," I said to Jehanne. "For France's sake, I will join you."

My wife looked at me, and I placed my right hand on her left one to let her know that it is ok. Jehanne said to my wife: "He'll be alright. No harm will come to him. He'll return to you safely."

"I'll pray to God for him," my wife said.

Jehanne said: "I was only three years old when the English king came to France."

"Yes," I said: "And he came again in 1417 and took Caen and Normandy. Rouen was not that easy to take, it gave in after a six month siege. Between the French and the English lines there were left thousands upon thousands of people dying of starvation. Three years later, King Charles VI asked for peace. This was then the treaty of Troyes where the Dauphin's mother, Isabeau of Bavaria, disowned him, she sided with the English. How could she have done such a terrible deed? Henry V was now given power over France while Charles was still alive, and the English line would get the French throne. Henry married Catherine, Charles VI's daughter, and from that union came Henry VI."

"Jehanne," my wife asked, "have you ever heard of the Bois Chesnu?"

Jehanne replied, "Yes, I have. It's an oak forest not far from my father's home."

"There's a prophecy about the oak forest and a maiden. There's also another prophecy about a woman who will bring France low, while a maiden would save it."

Jehanne said to my wife, "I have heard about these prophecies but I pay no heed to them. I just listen to my council from heaven. They direct me in what I should do. So, I will continue telling the story of what happened when I left Domremy. For a second time I went back to see Robert de Baudricourt, he turned me down, would not listen to me. Then I finally went back to him for the third time, he actually listened to me. I told him about the French being defeated at the battle of Rouvray, just outside of Orléans. No news had come as yet to Vaucouleurs; it was my voices who informed me of the event. Then Robert believed in me."

"That battle," I told Jehanne, "was known as the *Battle of the Herrings*. It was a disastrous day for France; and for the soldiers who had to go to Orléans to break the siege."

"Tell me what happened. My voices had told me that France got defeated, but not how."

"It was close to Lent," I started telling her, "when a convoy of about 300 wagons were on their way from Paris to the siege of Orléans. The convoy was commanded by John Fastolf. The wagons had all sorts of things on them such as many barrels of herrings. The soldiers had to eat fish at Lent. There were also long-bow arrows, gunpowder, and other items. The convoy had about 1,000 archers or more escorting it. When it reached the village of Rouvray, not far from Janville, they stopped and settled in for the night. As morning broke, the French advanced guards were seen. John Fastolf immediately got the wagons in a defensive way with two openings. At one opening, were the archers, and at the other, were the sharp stakes. The French had more soldiers than the English. They outnumbered them 3-1. The French kept on advancing, closing in on the English. Clermont, the French commander, stopped the van. He decided that they should not dismount. The gunners and cross-bow men started bombarding the wagons. The English were getting hammered, the gunfire was causing much damage. The French cannon could not reach to the English long-bow men. Scottish commander, John Stewart Darnley did not pay any attention to the orders given by Clermont. He had his men dismount, and then they started advancing to the wagons. As soon as they were in range of the English long-bow men they got slaughtered. Clermont had his mounted men-at-arms to launch a follow-on charge. It did not go well for them. The English commander seeing the disastrous confusion the French and Scots were in, sent out the few men-at-arms he had in a counter attack. Soon the French army was destroyed. Stewart was killed along with 120 knights and 600 others. Clermont got wounded, many others as well."

"One mistake can be very dangerous for the rest of the men-at-arms. That's why it is very important that everyone knows exactly what they are supposed to do," Jehanne said.

It was now getting close to noon, time to have lunch. We all had something to eat, and talked some more about France. I said that if Orléans falls, the Dauphin would lose everything. The English would have total control of France. My wife said to

Jehanne, "It must have been a long and tedious journey for you coming all the way from Vaucouleurs to Chinon; and then with the area infested with the English and Burgundian soldiers."

Jehanne said: "When I first entered Vaucouleurs, I talked with Jean de Metz who believed what I was saying, and promised to take me to Chinon. Robert Poulengy volunteered too. Robert de Baudricourt decided that it was right to send me and so started making preparations. There were also four others who joined in, and we left Vaucouleurs late in the evening. The people of Vacouleurs gave me a horse, and then I got clothing from the servant of Jean de Metz. I got hose, breeches, a tunic, doublet and a sword from Robert. It was the 23rd February when the six of us went out the gate. We rode in the night time a lot, and rested in the daytime. Our first stop was St. Urbaine, an old Abbey. I even got to Mass in Auxerre. Jean de Metz and I slipped in the city without anyone recognizing us, and we came out safely again. Then we got to Saint Catherine Fierbois. There, my voices told me about a sword that was hidden behind the high altar. As soon as I got in this place of Tours, I asked the armourer to go and fetch that sword for me. They gave two sheaths with the sword, and I had another one made of leather, the proper thing to do, I thought so at the time. From Saint Catherine Fierbois, I sent the Dauphin a letter to let him know where I was; and that I was on my way to him. It was later on the 6th of March that I finally got to see the king."

I said: "Çhinon is on the Vienne river. Theobald I, Count of Blois was the first to build a castle there in the 10th century. He used it as a stronghold. It changed hands many times, and the house of Anjou occupied it at one time."

Jehanne continued: "I stayed at the tower of Coudray with a bridge leading to the rest of the castle. I was visited by Lady Gaucourt and Lady Treves. I remember that when I was going up to the castle from the inn where I had stayed, a man on horseback came along, he saw me and said, "My God, is that the Maid?" He kept on insulting me. I said to him, "Do you blaspheme God? You who are so near your death?" Later on, the man fell into the water and was drowned."

I said to Jehanne, "The curse of God fell on him. It was his own fault insulting a young girl sent by God to rescue France!"

Jehanne said, "Yes, by my faith, he deserves what he got, but it made me sad. I wished he had confessed before he died."

I said, "It's not your fault that it happened that way."

Jehanne said: "And then I entered the castle into a room filled with many people, and there was this man sitting in the king's chair. My voices had already told me about the king. So I said, "Where is the real king?" Everyone was amazed when I said so. I started looking around the room, and then I saw the king, a few metres from me talking with a small group of people. I went over, fell on my knee, held his leg in my hand, and said, "Gentle Dauphin, I've been sent to you from the king of heaven. My name is Jehanne la Pucelle. I have come to take Orléans back, being now surrounded by the English, and also to take you to Riems for your coronation.""

I said to Jehanne, "Why did you pick that name?"

"You know Jean, I am a simple girl, and I have given myself to God; so I am the little Maid."

"Sounds solid," I remarked.

"Anyway, to carry on, some of the officials, after some discussion among themselves, took me into another room so that I could talk privately with the Dauphin. When I was finally alone with him, I told him things that no one else in the world knew about, except God. From that moment on, the Dauphin believed me, but he still had a worried look upon his face. He believed that I was sent from God."

"What was the secret, Jehanne?" I tried to fish it out of her.

"No, Jean, not even you would get to know what it is. There are some revelations that are only meant for the king. And I received many revelations about the Duke of Orléans as well."

"Ok! Carry on."

"The Dauphin still wasn't satisfied. He had some of the churchmen there at hand, to examine me by asking many questions which I answered well. Late on, they took me to Poitiers for three weeks for more examinations and questions from the learned theologians. They did not find anything to accuse me of, and they told the Dauphin so. They found everything about me was positive. It was told to the Dauphin that he can go ahead and place me to lead his troops in Orléans. In Poitiers I dictated a letter to the English commanders at Orléans. It went something like this:

3.

Blois and Orléans

It was time now to leave Tours and move on to Blois and then on to Orléans. First, Jehanne had to be kitted out with armour in Tours before she moved to Blois to meet the soldiers who would be fighting with her to rescue Orléans.

~

King of England, and you Duke of Bedford, who call yourself Regent of the kingdom of France; you, William de la Pole, Earl of Suffolk; John, Lord of Talbot; and you, Thomas, Lord Scales, who call yourselves Bedford's Lieutenants, do right by the king of Heaven. Hand over to the Maiden, who is sent here by God the king of Heaven, the keys to all the towns which you have taken and violated in France. She has come here in the name of God to support the Royal family. She is quite prepared to make peace, if you are willing to do right, so long as you give up France and make amends for occupying it. And you archers, soldiers both noble and otherwise, who are around the town of Orléans, in God's name go back to your own lands. And if you will not do so await word of the Maiden, who will go to see you soon to your very great misfortune. King of England, if you do not do so, I am a commander, and wherever I come across your troops in France, I shall make them go. I will have them wipe out. I am sent here by God the King of Heaven – an eye for an eye – to drive you entirely out of France. And if they are willing to obey, I shall have mercy on them. And do not think otherwise, for you will never hold the kingdom of France from God the King of Heaven, the son of Saint Mary; king Charles, the true heir, will hold it; for God the King of Heaven wills it; and this has been revealed by the Maiden to him (Charles) who shall enter Paris with a fine contingent of troops. If you do not believe the tidings sent by God and the Maiden, wherever we find you we will strike against you and will cause such a great clash of arms there that not for a thousand years has France seen one as great, if you do not do right. And firmly believe that the King of Heaven will send greater force to the Maiden than you would be able to bring against her and her good men-at arms in all of your assaults. And in the fighting we shall see who has the better right (whether God of Heaven or you). Duke of Bedford, the Maiden asks and requests that you will not cause your own downfall. If you will do right, you could yet come in her company to where the French will do the noblest deed which has ever been done for Christianity. And reply if you wish to make peace in the city of Orléans; and if you do not do so, you will shortly contemplate your great misfortunes. Written this Tuesday in Holy Week.

"Jehanne," I said, "I know you from childhood days, we spoke to each other about many things. But I must say that this letter is not of your own doing. There are some words in it that you would not have dictated."

"I know," Jehanne confirmed. "It is Jean Erault who wrote what I dictated. There are indeed some things in it that I did not say."

"And you must think of the English, they're not new at this game. They are hardened soldiers; and they do not scare easily. I don't think that they will take your letter seriously. I know you, but they don't know you. They'll be thinking: 'Who is this Maid?'"

"I know, those Godons are mad, full of swearing; and they think that they can take France. They will not have her."

I said, "Jehanne, in 1424 there was a very bloody battle: it was a very important battle. The Scots fighting with the French lost about 4,000 men. Over 7,000 French and her allies were killed. Both of the Scots commanders were killed: Archibald, Earl of Douglas and John Stewart, Earl of Buchan. The English only lost about 1600. After that battle, the army of Scotland were no longer available to play a part in the hundred years war. Still, many Scottish soldiers stayed on and kept fighting with France.

The Duke of Bedford had laid siege to Ivry near LeMans. With a strong Scots and French forces, they set out to relieve it. Ivry gave themselves over to the English before the Scots and French got there. A war council was held and the French decided to attack English strongholds in Southern Normandy starting with Verneuil. The Scots secured Verneuil by pretending to be Englishmen escorting Scottish prisoners – they were admitted to the fortified place – and safely took charge. The Duke of Bedford when he learned what had taken place, got troops and hurried to Verneuil. The Scottish soldiers told the French that they must stay and fight.

The battle started on August 17th. The battle was fought along the lines of Crecy and Agincourt. The French broke through and went straight for the baggage train; the French infantry were defeated. Bedford had made sure that the train was protected by a force of 2,000 long-bow men, they turn back the cavalry. A long battle was fought, and the English were the winners. Alencon was captured and many others."

"The French did a foolish thing in trying to attack the baggage train first," Jehanne told me. "That's why they were defeated. We must not let such a thing happen whenever we're in the field, and have to make battle line."

I said, "They had enough forces to stand up to the English, but through bad tactics, they made a mess of it."

Jehanne said to me: "From what you told me, this battle was horrid, it was vicious, and it was bloody. But the battle we are going to fight at Orléans would turn out different. *We* have to get the besiegers out; and to do that we have to scale ladders; we have to get up unto the rampart; we have to be brave and bold."

"Of course," I answered back. "When are you going to send that letter to the English?"

"When I get to Blois, and I'm on my way to Orléans," Jehanne said, "I shall send one of my heralds with it."

"So what happened after all the examinations at Poitiers?" I asked her.

She said: "I had to go to Tours to be fitted out with armour; and here I am talking with you, my childhood friend. You mentioned that Alencon got captured in the battle at Verneuil!"

"That's right. He had to pay a great sum for ransom."

Jehanne told me: "I met him at Chinon. He is my noble Duke. He is a great man. He gave me a horse after he saw how good I was with a lance."

"All those practices we had with those sticks, Jehanne, you're now an expert."

"I actually enjoyed what we did playing with those sticks – playing at being soldiers – pretending that we were actually in battle. Well, I'm now here in Tours and soon will be kitted out, we shall all go down to the armourer."

An hour later I was there with Jehanne and her little group at the armourer. She said to me when we first arrived there, "Ah! I do hope that they fit me out well." As soon as she had spoken, a messenger came on horse and told Jehanne that she was invited to visit Duke d'Alencon at his castle. He told her the date. She must take the boat down the Loire to Saumur and St. Laurent, and from there on horse to the castle. Jehanne thanked the messenger. She was then fitted out with a brand new shining armour without any engravings on it. It was just plain. I also got fitted out with one, but less expensive. The others in the group had armour too. I was amazed to see Father Pasquerel without one. He had this thing like a band around his forehead that made him look like one that was bald. He had sandals on his feet. From the armourer, we went to the Scottish painter where Jehanne got her banner and pennon. "This is really good," she said. "Our Lord high and sitting on a rainbow." She was very happy with the work and she told the painter so.

On the 21st April I bid farewell to my parents, wife and young son, and left Tours with Jehanne and her military household, a group of soldiers, all shouting with much noise, as we left for Blois. We pass through Marmoutiers, Sanit Radegonde, Roch Corbon, Vouvray, Vernon, Noizay, Nazelle Onzain and Chouzy S Lisse. The day was a nice sunny day.

Just after getting our armour, Jehanne had paid a visit to the duke d'Alencon. When she came back she said that she enjoyed the visit, and that they had been hunting quails. She said that the castle was very big and that there were many horse there. She said that she enjoyed chatting with the duke's mother and his wife.

Blois is not a very large place. It is situated on the Loire River. It has a very old castle where some famous kings were accomodated. Blois is a place vety much hated by the Jews because of the cruelty they suffered there in 1171. The Jews at that time had many enemies; and these enemies would go out their way and make all sort of accusations against them. It got out of hand when the accusators accused the Jews of needing Christian blood for their Passover; and for other secret rituals. This accusation first started in Norwich, in

England, in the year of 1144. Then it was followed on in other cities. Then it spread to Europe. There is a story recorded; and it goes like this:

In the year 1171 there lived about 40 Jews in Blois. One of them whose name was Isaac ben Eleazar rode up to the river one Thursday, toward evening, just before Pesach. A stable servant rode up at the same time to water the horse of his master. The Jew bore on his chest an untanned hide; but one of the corners had become loose and was sticking out his coat. When, in the gloom, the servant's horse saw the white side of the hide, it was frightened and sprang back, and it could not be brought to water. The Christian servant was a simple peasant, who had often heard the priest preach in church that Jews used Christian blood for their passover matzoth and wine, warning all his flock to keep a watchful eye over their children during the passover season. Now, when his horse took fright, he hastened back to his master and said: "Hear, my lord, what a certain Jew did. As I rode behind him toward the river in order to give your horse a drink, I saw him throw a little Christian child, whom the Jews have killed, into the water. When I saw this I was horrified and hastened back quickly for fear he might kill me too. Even the horse under me was so frightened by the splash of water, when he threw the child in it, that it would not drink."

The servant knew that his master would rejoice at the misfortune of the Jews, because he hated a certain Jewess, influential in the city. He was not mistaken for his master said: "Now I can have my vengeance on that woman and the rest of the Jews." The next morning the master rode to the ruler of the city, Theobald, son of Theobald, Count of Blois (son-in-law of King Louis VII of France). The Christians called him

"The Good," but he was a wicked, cruel man. When the ruler heard the accusation he became enraged and had all the Jews of Blois seized and thrown into prison, and all put into iron chains. The only exception was that influential Jewish woman, Dame Pulcelina, whom the Count admired for her wisdom and beauty. She had often been able to get favours from the ruler for the Jewish merchants of Blois. But now, the Count's wife (Alix, daughter of the king) gave strict orders to the servants not to allow her to speak to her husband for fear she might get him to change his mind. The ruler had no evidence against the Jews, except for that half-wit stable servant.

The Count was ready to make a deal with the Jews and free them for a large sum of ransom money. He sent a Jew to the neighbouring communities, to ask them how much they would give to free their brethren. The Jews consulted with the imprisoned hostages, and the latter advised offering only one hundred pounds, in addition to their uncollected debts from Christian debtors amounting to the sum of one hundred and eighty pounds. The Jews in the dungeon told their brethren in other communities not to pay a high ransom for their lives, lest the Christians should find it profitable to imprison Jews for ransom. However, nothing came of the negotiations because the Bishop arrived on the scene and insisted that the Jews should be condemned to die, and that he would 'prove' their guilt. The priest told the Count to have the witness tested by the ordeal of water, to discover if he had told the truth. The test was to be arranged as follows: A huge tank would be filled with water, and the servant who 'saw' the Jew throw the child into the water would be put into it – if he floated, his words were true, if he sank, he had lied. The Count of Blois commanded that the test be carried out forthwith.

Now the priest had so arranged in advance that the servant should not sink in the water. Such was the justice in those days. The Jews were found guilty on the basis of that water, and condemned to be burned alive. At the wicked ruler's command they were taken and put into a wooden house around which were placed thornbushes and faggots. As they were led forth, they were told, "You can save your lives if you leave your religion and accept ours." The Jews refused. They were beaten and tortured to make them accept the Christian religion, but still they refused. Rather, they encouraged each other to remain steadfast and die for the sanctification of God's name.

At the Count's command two of the leading Jews, both Kohanim, Rabbi Yechiel, the son of Rabbi David ha Kohen, and Rabbi Yekuthiel, the son of Rabbi Jadah ha Kohen, were taken and tied to a single stake to be burned in front of the others, so as to make the others convert. They were both saintly and pious men of great Torah learning, being the disciples of Rabbeinu Yaakov Tam and Rabbeinu Shmuel ben Meir, them grandson of Rashi. A third prominent Jew, Rabbi Judah, the son of Aaron was also tied with them to the stake. At the ruler's command, fire was set to the faggots. The fire spread to the cords on their hands so that they snapped. The three Jews came out of the fire and called to the Christians who had assembled to watch them die. "By your own laws you should set us free, for you see that we came out alive from the ordeal of fire!" They struggled to get out, but they were overpowered and pushed back into the house, and the house was set on fire. They came out again and seized one of the executioners and dragged him along with them towards the fire. When they were right at the fire, the armed soldiers pulled themselves together, rescued the

Christians from their hands, killed them with their swords, and then threw their bodies into the fire.

A certain Jew by the name of Rabbi Baruch ben David ha Kohen was there and saw all this at that time with his own eyes. He lived in the territory of that ruler and had come there to arrange terms for the release of the Jews of Blois, but unfortunately, he did not succeed. However, a settlement was made by him for one thousand pounds to save the other Jews of that accursed ruler. He also saved the scrolls of the Torah and other sacred books.

We arrived at Blois where Duke d'Alencon was in charge of operations to Orléans. Jehanne was taken to the place where the captains lodged. Each captain had his coat of arms displayed before his tent. It was very colourful with all the blues, reds, greens, yellows, blacks and whites. It didn't take long for the news to get around that the *Maid* had arrived. All the captains assembled in the usual area... there was at first lots of noise and shouting, and then suddenly it died down. Everyone was staring. Jehanne got down from her black charger. Duke d'Alencon said: "Men, this here is *The Maid*. You have heard a lot about her coming to the Dauphin, and to break the siege of Orléans. Take a good look. She is real. Now pay attention and listen carefully to what she has to say." The duke introduced Jehanne to the Marshall of his forces, the Baron Ambroise de Lore. The Dauphin had given Ambroise the task to assist the duke with organizing this army of reinforcement as well as to escort Jehanne to Orléans.

As all the other soldiers gathered round, one captain became angry, and behaved badly interrupting de Loire's conversation with Jehanne. He held her in contempt for being considered his superior when she was only a peasant woman. He shouted out, "Well, my brother knights, since it is your desire to follow this low-born wench, this geuse, rather than someone of my standing, I shall not stop you! Henceforth, I shall not play my part as a knight, but will serve only as a humble squire. Yet I would much prefer to have a nobleman for my master and not this peasant woman, *nobody!*"

Jehanne, when she heard that, went and stood before him face to face. "Go or stay," she said. "It matters not to me. What matters is that God's will be accomplished." Then she turned her back on him.

Duke d'Alencon had to do something quickly in order to get peace. He turned to Jehanne and said, "Come on friends! We are here to do battle against the Godons, not each other. Come now, Gemaches, Jehanne, embrace and make peace."

Jehanne and Gemaches were still angry with each other. Then the duke dragged them together, and they half-heartedly shook hands.

"Now we are all friends again," the duke said, as Gemaches turned and walked away.

Supplies were coming in ready to be transported to Orléans where food was getting short. It was vitally important for the supplies to get there on time so that the people would not starve, and then turn themselves over to the English instead. Jehanne stood up on a small podium and said: "I welcome all of you who are willing to fight for the Dauphin and for France. I was sent by the King of Heaven to do two things: one, to get the English to retreat from Orléans: two, to take our noble Dauphin to Riems and have him crowned. Inside this camp, there'll be no more swearing, drinking, looting, gambling, and camp followers. Either you marry your lover or they must leave."

"Wait a minute, here!" The man with the limp came closer, looked up at her. "You have to be joking by saying no more swearing and drinking! What has a soldier got left than these? We need these things to keep us going."

"Who are you?" she asked.

"I am La Hire, and I do swear and drink a lot. How am I to stop just like that? No soldier will take what you're saying seriously."

"If you want to have victory over the English, you will have to follow my instructions, for that is the only sure way to show yourselves as righteous soldiers – then you'll get the victory – the victory God has promised you. All I ask is that you all confess your sins and go to mass regularly."

There was a black-haired, good-looking soldier, with a beard, strong and able. He said: "Everyone has sins, and they crop up daily. Is your talking as good as your fighting?"

"Daily you will have to confess your sins, that's all I am asking. When we get to Orléans, you can judge for yourself, if I'm good in fighting or not."

There was mumbling and grumbling amongst the soldiers. They did not like what had been said. It was too harsh.

Jehanne said: "I want to see you all at mass tomorrow morning, and if you do not turn up, I'll leave you and go back to my parents, and look after the sheep."

Jehanne was shown around the whole camp. It was really in a terrible state with all the camp followers, and all the shouting and bad language everywhere you turn. I was now thinking that this Jehanne had done well for herself, having her own household, two pages, two heralds, a personal bodyguard; and all the trimmings to go with it. I learn that she had been given the title *War Chief,* – she was the visionary leader – she was the one to keep the troops spiritually fed. Jean d'Aulon, I noticed, was a very good soldier; he was honest, he made sure no harm came to Jehanne. There was one soldier there that I just didn't take a liking to. He was a tall, well-built man with black hair whose name I later found out was Gilles de Rais. La Hire, and I got on well, he was a hardened soldier – a mercenary. I was told that he came from the area of Gascon. I noticed that he had a limp. There were other great noble soldiers aaround, I didn't get to meet them all on that first day; but later on, as time passed, I got to know them more.

I went to my tent and later on went to the tent of Jehanne where she was about to meet some Scottish soldiers. These soldiers had been fighting in small groups helping France as mercenaries. Their country was no longer in the 100 years war, and most of them had gone back to Scotland.

4.

Preparing for Orléans

Jehanne is at Blois. She told the troops that she was sent to rid Orléans of the English and to crown the Dauphin at Riems. Preparations are being made to leave Blois and enter Orléans.

~

Jehanne had a very large tent with left side and right side space. There were braziers within. In front of the tent there was an antichamber leading in to the main part of the tent. I got there just in time to meet Patrick Ogilvy. He was also in charge of seeing that the operation to Orléans went okay. He was Constable of the Scottish soldiers. There were other Scottish commanders already there. I said to Jehanne that whenever she heard the word "lass" from any of the Scottish soldiers, that it meant a young girl or young woman. Some of the commanders said that Scottish troops came to Orléans in 1428, and that some got killed when the English had first laid siege to the city. Another name came up – it was William Hamilton. I broke in and said: "It was a man by that same name "William" who got Scotland back her freedom. He was a great hero, stood up against the odds, giving Edward I a run for his money."

"Aye," said Patrick Ogilvy. "He was a brave one, that William Wallace, pity that he was betrayed. Edward captured him and had him hanged, beheaded and disemboweled."

We talked some more about the affairs of Scotland, and then turned to the affairs of France. Jehanne learned later on that another meeting in another tent took place and she wasn't invited. There, they had thrashed out the moving to Orléans; and how to tackle the outlying English forts, then eventually the Tourelles itself. She was very angry. She told me that she would speak to them about it in the morning after mass. Staying a while longer paying tribute to the Scots and then she turned in. I went back over to my tent, lit a small fire to keep me warm for it got colder, had a drink, then I drifted off to sleep.

Everyone was up and refreshed in the morning. All the commanders, nobles, knights and squires, barons and counts along with the soldiers were treading over towards the priests to confess their sins and to hear mass sung. Jehanne had warned them that if they did not turn up, she would leave them. They wanted her to stay so they all turned out. Father Pasquerel had made a pennon with the crucifix upon it, and there, the priests all gathered. It was amazing to see La Hire and Gilles de Rais, and even that Jean Gamaches, all there ready to confess their sins. Jehanne was pleased that they all turned up. They believed in her, and she wasn't going to let them down. She knew too, that when they all had finished confessing their sins, they would be pure from all the bad things that they were accustomed of doing. And she knew, without a doubt, that they were now capable to thrash the English.

After confessions and mass, we all started preparing and packing up ready to leave Blois. Everyone knew that Jehanne was a woman wearing men's clothing to protect herself. No one had any trouble with that – they knew without a doubt who she was – she was their head. There are some women who disguise themselves as men, and the men in their group haven't even a clue that there was a woman among them. I remembered when I was at her tent last night, she had said to me that she wants to hear much more of the history of Scotland. She knew that that was my subject and that I was very good in it. She had told me too, that back at home her mother had told her about lots of things that had taken place.

Medieval fighting is not an easy thing; it is cruel, bloody, vicious; some men are taken for ransom while others are slain. There are many laws drawn up for this sort of fighting. If an army don't want to fight you at a certain time, they will just let you know. Sometimes they follow each other for days on end, trying to find a weak point where they attack and gain the victory. If battle lines are drawn, then you had better be good at what you do, for there is the cavalry that come charging at you. And you have the archers with their pointed stakes which they drive in the ground to halt the charging cavalry. You also have the cannons, and the foot soldiers.

One goes into this melee very boldly and couradeously. You go in fighting your way, and hoping that you come back out again. You have to go down into moats and scale ladders in order to get to the first ramparts. If the moats are very deep, they have to be filled up with faggots bundled up and ready, you throw anything that you do not want, that is at hand, down into the moat. Once on the rampart, you have to fight your way up to a new height using more ladders. You take a break while fresh soldiers take over. Sometimes an attack could last from morning to evening without stopping.

On the morning when all the army went to confession and mass, only those soldiers who confessed was allowed to hear mass. Jehanne did have some words with some of the captains for not telling her about the council which they had held the night the Scottish soldiers were with her. They told her that it was very important and has to be kept a secret for their attack on the English. She told them that she can keep a secret and that she too have a council. They promised to let her in at the next council.

It was now 25th April, time for us to leave Blois and head towards Orléans. There were many people cheering lining the streets, others looked down from their windows along the way. The priests were in the front carrying banners and chanting the *Veni Creator Spiritus!* Behind them was Jehanne and her army of about 4,000 men on their chargers. Next was her household staff. Jean d'Aulon was on a horse with a special saddle, called a *Banner Saddle*. Raymond had Jehanne's pennon. Behind were many wagons with all sorts of tools for war. From Blois we passed Bracieux, Dhuizon, Villeny, Ligny le Ribault, Ujouy le Poiter, Ardon, La Source, Olivet and then Crecy.

Jehanne did not know where Orléans was situated. The escort, she knew would take her there, that was their job. She wanted as soon as she got there to engage the English, she did not want to waste any time. For the first time she had slept in her armour, and felt the bruises from it. She got use to it after a while. Jehanne came immediately to see that the river was between herself and Orléans. She was not at all pleased that such a thing had taken place. She wanted to know who was responsible to let such a thing happen – to trick her. The Bastard, who was in charge of Orléans had already left to come and meet us. When he saw Jehanne, he greeted her. "I am glad that you arrived safely," he said.

"Are you the Bastard?" she asked. "Why did they bring me on this side of the river? Can I fight the English here on this side?"

The Bastard said, "I know that you cannot reach the English from here, but it was orders from the authorities for our safety."

Jehanne told him, "You've been to your council, and I have been to mine, now let's see which one is right."

The Bastard was a very good commander, he knew how to treat Jehanne, he knew that she was also a good soldier and very religious. Whenever she would get into a temper, he knew immediately what to do. In that way, he eased the tension between them both.

There were only a few barges, not enough to take all the troops and goods across the river. It was decided then that some of the troops should return to Blois along with the priests. Jehanne was furious, she did not want to be parted from her soldiers. But it was explained to her properly the reason why that had to be so. She finally accepted what was planned by the captains. We had to wait a while because the river was low and the wind had changed direction. Jehanne told us that it would be okay. We then crossed over and it was getting on close to eight in the evening when we entered Orléans. Jehanne on a white horse in her shining armour with the Bastard on her left side, Jean d'Aulon on her right, with La Hire just behind him with the other captains and squires following.

The Scots pipers played a tune as we entered Orléans. I wasn't very far behind riding between her two brothers, Pierre and Jean. There was lots of shouting in the streets, people rushing forward to have a good look at Jehanne. We finally got to the house where Jehanne would stay with the Boucher family. His daughter's name was Charlotte. He was the treasurer of the Duke of Orléans. The Duke of Orléans was one of those who had been taken captive at Agincourt.

Jehanne was tired from all the travelling and meeting with all the officials. She had already sent her heralds Guienne and Ambleville with a letter to the English. She was asking them to pack up and leave – go back to their own country – and leave France alone. The English had not taken the letter seriously, they only scowled her more. They had sent back Ambleville, and kept Guienne ready to burn him. Jehanne had told Ambleville to go back to the English because they would not lay a hand on him, and that he would return with Guienne. The English had already erected a stake so that they could burn Guienne; but first, they had to write to the University of Paris to explain what they were about to do. There had been laws laid down that a herald was sancrosanct.

On April 30th, La Hire and Florent de Illiers, with a large force of men-at-arms, attacked an English outpost just by the fort of Paris and the city wall, they drove the men back into the main work. There was the sound of artillery fire back and forth but nothing much happened. When it was evening, Jehanne summoned Glasdale to leave the Tourelles in peace. The English shouted back across the river insulting her with all sorts of names. They said that if they should catch her, they would burn her. On Sunday 1st May Dunois (the Bastard of Orléans), with enough soldiers, and with Jean d' Aulon rode away to Blois. The Bastard went to make sure that all the troops that had returned to Blois were available to depart for Orléans. Jehanne and La Hire made cover for the Bastard when he left Orléans. On this same day, Jehanne rode through the streets with knights and squires. The people were eager to see her. Monday 2nd May 1429, Jehanne went out the gate of Orléans with a great number of people following her. She examines the English positions without any one hindering her. On the 3rd May troops came from the garrisons of Montargis, Chateau-Regnard and Gien. News came in that the army from Blois was near. Jehanne went out at dawn with about 500 troops under La Hire to meet them the oncoming soldiers, and again, no one bothered them. It is strange that none of the English commanders made a move to try and prevent us from entering Orléans. By noon, all the troops were in the city.

Jehanne was dining with d'Aulon when the Bastard came in with news: Fastolf who defeated the Scots and French at Rouvray (the Battle of Herrings), was coming from Paris, and was now in Janville, a day's march away, with reinforcements and supplies for the English. Jehanne was smiling when she heard the news. "In God's name, Bastard, I command you to let me know as soon as you hear of Fastolf's arrival. If he passes without my knowledge, I ... will have your head!"

"For that fear not," said the Bastard, "for I shall let you have news as soon as it arrives." Then he left.

Jehanne was very tired, she went and laid down beside her hostess on a bed, while d'Aulon who was also fatigued laid down on a sofa, in the same room. None of us knew that an attack was being organised against St. Loup, an English fort far outside the remotest gate of Orléans. I was also on a sofa not far from d'Aulon. I needed this rest badly after the day's events. I was dozing off when suddenly Jehanne jumped up and asked to be armed. She said, "My voices told me that I should attack now, but I don"t know if I should go against the English in the fort, or Fastolf who is on his way to the English."

I told her to take that which was nearest. She accepted and hurriedly got her armour on with the help of d'Aulon and the hostess. I quickly got help as well and was ready. As we went down the stairs, she met up with the page, Louis Coutes. She said to him, "Ah! Why didn"t you tell me that there was French blood spilling? Go and fetch my horse." When he had done that, she told him to get her banner. He passed it to her through the window.

No sooner had she got it she was away towards the Burgundy gate. D'Aulon was still half dressed with his armour, but he got on his horse and followed her. Louis Coutes, her page followed behind me.

When Jehanne reached the place where all the French troops were, she saw many wounded and was angry. The English were getting themselves ready to stop any force that should come against them. Jehanne advanced against the English with great force; and with haste. When the French saw her they were glad and started shouting, and in a while the Fort of St. Loup was taken. The English priests all came and stood before Jehanne. She saw to it that no harm came to them. She took them all back to where she was lodging. The rest of the English were killed by the people of Orléans.

Jehanne never ate regularly. Often she would dip a piece of bread in some wine; and that would be it for the rest of the day. I often wondered where she got the strength from to go through the day; through strenuous battles; without fainting, for lack of energy. I decided not to ask her about it. I heard from religious people that they get some sort of spiritual power that cannot be explained to others.

The next day we went out through a side gate with the soldiers belonging to the king, and then we crossed the river by boats joined to each other. Before us was the Fort of St. Jean-le-Blanc. We attacked it, then went immediately to another fort near the Augustins. The King's soldiers were in trouble so Jehanne shouted: "Let us advance boldly, In God's name."

Another day, we crossed over the river, having our horses in a boat. As soon as we got to where we wanted to go, we mounted; La Hire and Jehanne with their lances at the ready. The English were just about to move forward upon the French when Jehanne and La Hire, who were always in the front to protect the French, couched their lances and were the first to attack the enemy. The rest of the soldiers followed suit. There was another time when we crossed, Jehanne and La Hire leading. The English soldiers who had the fort of Saint-le Blanc, saw how great a force was crossing over the river, so they abandoned the fort and went over to that of Saint Augustins. After much fighting, the fort of saint Augustins was taken by the French. The captains told Jehanne that she should return to Orléans, she refused, saying: "Shall we leave our men?" Later, with the French troops and her page, we crossed the river, and entered Orléans.

The next day some of the King's followers were espoused to too great a danger. The captains had said that they will not attack because of too few troops, they wanted to wait for reinforcement, Jehanne said to them, "You have been with your council, and I have been with mine. Believe me, my council will hold good and will accomplished what it set out to do. Yours will come to nothing." She informs Pasquerel, her confessor, "Get up early tomorrow morning even earlier than you did today, and do the best you can. You must stay near me all the time, for tomorrow I have much to do more than I ever had yet, and the blood will flow from my body above my breast."

I said to her: "Have you got enough troops to make an attack tomorrow?"

"The captains do not think so. They say we should wait for more reinforcement; but I say that we should attack immediately."

"Have you thought it through properly?" I asked her. "Can you really win against the English?"

"Jean," she said, "I know that we are going to drive the English away, no matter how many troops we have. My council told me that I would win, and I believe what they have told me. We've had extra forces come in from garrisons, and I think that should be enough."

"Alright, Jehanne. I am with you all the way, but your captains are hesitating."

Jehanne said: "They've been doing so for a long time; only those who believe in me will trust me."

5.

The Battle for Les Tourelles

Jehanne is set to attack the English main tower, Les Tourelles. Her captains, at that moment, do not agree with her. Jehanne is confident that she'll win and warned her confessor to stay near to her always. What she's taking on is really a hard thing to do.

The night before the battle for Les Tourelles, there were many high officials from the town in the house belonging to the Boucher's. The Bishop of Orléans was there as well, he was from Scotland. Charlotte was sitting next to me, and was longing for me to tell her about how France came to be. Jehanne was also interested to hear the story. When most of the guests had gone, and Charlotte was allowed to stay up as late as the others, I started telling them about the history of France. Around the table were Jean de metz, Father Pasquerei, Bertrand de Poulegny, Jacques Boucher and his wife, D'Aulon, Jehanne, her two brothers, Charlotte and one herald, Ambleville, and two pages. I was ready to start telling the history of France when Jacques Boucher said: "Our Duke of Orléans who was captured at Agincourt would have found it pleasurable to be here, and listening to how France came to be. Unfortunately, he is in the tower of London with years still to do."

D'Aulon said, "Great Lords and Barons and knights and men-at-arms lost their lives at that battle; but that will always happen when one is defending the country. Some of us have to give our lives to create a way forward."

Pierre said: "Whatever should happen tomorrow, I will be there in the heart of it. If my sister can be there, so could I."

Jean said: "Together, we'll struggle to free France from her enemies."

Pasquerel said: "I have seen quite a number of documents about the history of France. I am interested to hear about it from you."

Charlotte said: "I want to hear about King Clovis and his wife Clotilda!"

"I will get to him," I said, "but you"ll have to be patient."

Raymond, one of the pages, said; "He converted to Christianity because of his wife."

Jehanne said, humorously, "You can start telling the history, Jean. We're all waiting to hear it."

"France," I started, "was long ago called *Gaul*. There was a group of people known as the *Celts*, and were also known as Gauls. Another group of people known as the *Franks* were in charge of Gaul. There were quite a number of German tribes around at that time. They married with the Romans and Gauls (Celts who were living in the Roman part of Gaul, and from them came the French). People at the time spoke Latin when the Romans were rulers. The Franks (the German tribes became powerful). They spoke Gallic, a mixture of Latin.

In 493 AD the Franks took Christianity as their religion. In 121 BC, Southern France was in the power of France. The name was Provinc, 250 AD Saint Denis became patron saint of France. The Christians at that time were treated badly. German tribes went into France in 406 AD, and settled there. The Romans did all they could but could not get rid of them, The Germanic tribes let the Romans rule them. The Franks had control of Nothern France around 500 AD. Clovis ruled the Franks from 481-511 AD. He converted to Christianity to please his wife. Clovis was really the grandson of Merovich who was the leader of the tribe. The dynasty which was called the *Merovingians* lasted for a very long period – almost 200 years. Clovis was the son of Childerick and the Thuringian queen Basina. He took over from his father when he was only 15 years old. He was ruler of the Salian Franks and other Frankish groups. He took over many territories especially those from the Allemani, the Burgundians – your friends Jehanne."

"Territories were also taken from the Visigoths." Jehanne said: "You know well that I will have nothing to do with them. I know you mean it as fun; but truly, they're my enemies; and you read too, Clovis took their lands from them."

D'Aulon said: "Clovis was a real leader among all those other groups. He wasn't a soft person. He was really tough."

I continued: "He did marry a Catholic Burgundian princess named Clotilda, and had five children with her. She wanted him very much to convert to her faith. There was one time when he was fighting a battle, the odds were against him, but he won; and that led him to trust in the Christian God, and so he got baptized. It was the Bishop of Riems, Remigus who baptized him. It was here in Orléans that he organized a council with the Catholic bishops. He was a great king, warrior, hero, and was the founder of France. By the way, when he got baptized there were about 3,000 soldiers who got baptized as well. Quite a number of marriages took place between the Franks and the Roman/Gallic people. Clovis brought out the Salic law. This law had mainly to do with monetary compensation and lands; and most of all it prevented women from taking over the throne through dynastic line."

Jehanne broke in, "Ah! you see, what those men in those days have done. It wasn't a good thing that they did. What do you think, Father Pasquerel?"

"You're right, Jehanne. Women should be given the chance to prove themselves. Things are changing now."

"Paris became the capital city for Clovis," I carried on. "He later went against Southern France to try and capture it. Around 507 AD most of France belonged to him. He died in 511 AD and was buried in the church of the Holy Apostles that he had built in Paris; later his wife joined him. The first dynasty of the Frankish kings were called Merovingians. Brittany, Provence and Burgany had ways to support themselves. Many people travelled from England to Brittany around the 5th century. In the 7th century, the Merovingian kings were losing power slowly. They were known as 'the kings who did nothing'. Then a great and mighty powerful family called the *Carolingians* ruled France. The first of their kings was Pepin the Short. Charles Martel was the son of Pepin the Short. It was Martel who stopped the Islamic invasion of Europe. This battle took place at Poitiers. He made war too, against the Saxons and Bavarians. The grandson of Charles Martel was Charlemagne, who later formed a great European Empire. No pagan at that time was safe. They were forced to convert to Christianity. In 800 AD Charlemagne became emperor and was crowned by the Pope. When Charlemagne died, Louis the Pius took charge in 814 AD, he died in 840 AD."

"So where I got examined by the learned doctors," Jehanne said, "there was this great battle! How strange that his name too, is Charles, just like the Duke of Orléans; and just like the Dauphin."

"There's only 680 years forward to your birth," I said. "Louis the Pious' sons made the treaty of Verdun in 843 AD. The territories of the Franks were split into three. The western part was ruled by Charles the Bald from 833-877 AD, then it became a part of France. Around the 8th century there was much trouble from the Arabs with the intention of ruling France. There was also the Vikings in the 9th and 10th centuries. But the French kings hadn't the power to stop them, and so there was dispute with the local magnates who protected the people. In 911 Charles the Simple made a treaty with the Viking king, Rollo. He was given Normandy for converting to Christianity, and to serve Charles faithfully. Hugh Capet became king in the year 987 AD. The French kings were kings with not much power to steer France. The Counts and Dukes didn't rely on any one. The Capetian kings only ruled a small piece of territory around Paris. The Duke of Normandy captured England, and under the feudal system, he was second to the French king. But because he was King of England. the Duke of Normandy was equal to the French king.

Henry, Count of Anjou married Eleanor of Aquitine. In 1154 AD he became King of England. Later, the kings of England took control of great parts of France. In 1202 AD the French King Phillip II went to war with the English King John, and he captured most of the lands in france, belonging to the English king. When Phillip II died, he had increased the area over which the French kings directly ruled. His grandson was Louis 9th (1226-1270 AD).

Deep into the 13th century the French kings had control og most of France The English had Aquitaine and Brittany and Burgundy; they were semi-independent. Phillip the Fair 1285-1314 AD extended the French kings control to the east by purchase and marriage. Things now were going right for France. Many universities were founded; Paris in 1150 AD; Toulouse 1229 AD; Montpellier 1289 AD; Avignon 1303 AD; Orléans 1306 AD; and Angers in 1337 AD.

Charles the Fair was the last Capetian king, he died in 328 AD. His cousin, Phillip of Valois became Phillip VI. Edward

III of England made the claim for the throne of France through his mother who was King Charles the Fair's sister. (Salic law did not allowed him to inherit the throne through a woman). In the year 1337 AD the hundred years war started. Many of the kings had connection with France leading back to William the Conqueror."

After I had finished with the quick history of France, every one started clapping. They said that they enjoyed it. Charlotte was very pleased and stated that she had learned quite a lot. It was now time for us to be going to bed for the sun had already sunk below the horizon. We all turned in and called it a day. On my sofa, in the room where Jehanne and Charlotte and D'Aulon were, I tossed and turned for a while; then sleep found me, and I drifted away to that mysterious other world.

Early next morning, 7th May, we were all up. We had breakfast and then attended mass and confessed our sins. Jehanne addressed the troops: "My friends, my good friends, today we're going into battle against the Godons. Go in boldly and be not afraid. The King of Heaven will give us the victory. Without fail, we shall drive the enemy away. They have no right to be here in France. Trust in God; and do not give up. God be with you in our fight for France and the Dauphin."

The troops started shouting, "For France, for France." The Scottish pipers played a tune on their pipes, then Jehanne lifted her sword for the trumpeters to sound for battle attack.

Now we were off still with some of the captains not wanting to attack. Raoul Gaucourt was the governor of Orléans and he was in charge of the gate known as the *Burgundy Gate*. When we arrived there, he refused to open the gate. Jehanne said to him, "Whether you like it or not, we'll get out this gate. You are a bad man." When he saw the great crowd of citizens and soldiers behind her, he quickly opened the gate, and we went out. Then we were confronted by seven types of barricades that were set up to stop us from getting to the Tourelles. We came to a sort of wooden barricade about eight or nine feet high with a small drawbridge. There was a ditch very wide and very deep. It was very slippery and one had to be careful when one gets to it. Then there was the boulevard – from here, the English would throw whatever they had at hand, at us. A small wooden bridge extended from the boulevard on the right side, and the bastion's long drawbridge joined up with it.

The moat was dry and was about twenty feet deep. We had to use our ladders to get down; then we come to the bastion. This structure was of stone, and about forty feet high; it was the fortification of the Tourelles. When we got over this wall, we came into a sort of courtyard about one hundred feet square. On the opposite side of this courtyard, was a water-filled moat. A drawbrige was attached to the Tourelles. Some of our men were trying to get the bridge that was leading from the boulevard to the Tourelles, to try and torch it, by placing lighted barges beneath it. Jehanne was the first to reach the walls after faggots were placed to fill in the ditch. She called out to the English commander Glasdale for him to give himself up – he and his men. She reminded him of what he had said to her days earlier, his harsh words and the names he had called her. The fighting became hard and fierce. Men were falling from ladders they had placed against the walls, in order to climb up. The English were throwing down stone, hot pitch, battle axes, pikes and anything that were available. The archers too, were very busy with their crossbow bolts. The English used long poles to push our ladders away from the wall. We were like ants going up these ladders. When one man fell, the next man was there already climbing madly to get to the rampart. I was amazed to see Jehanne standing on the rampart – which was the first one – and holding fast unto her standard. All around her, men were fighting for their lives. The sound of cannons were constant, battle axes were crushing down on steel helmets (the head piece with its visor). Men were falling to the ground; and not rising up again. After the Palisade was broken down, and it was coming up for noon, the boulevard was in our hands, then we descended the walls from within the dry moat.

Jehanne, as she was climbing up a ladder, got hit with a crossbow bolt, just above the breast and into the shoulder, and she fell back to the ground. She was not very far up the ladder – a couple of rungs. She screamed, and I have never heard a scream like that before. It got to me, but I steadied myself. Tears came to her eyes. Jean de Gamaches was near to her when she got hit. I rushed over and said to her that she would be okay. Her page, Louis Coutes, took the breast plate off. Pasquerel was there, close by, he prayed for her healing. Many soldiers surrounded the area. We got her out of the range of the English archers. The battle had been going on for a long time. It started at seven in the morning. There were heaps of men and ladders on the ground, some of them had no life at all, others crawled out and got themselves back into the fight. Jehanne's wound was dressed with olive oil. She rested for a while and was back into action. It was getting late now, and we were all really tired. The Bastard sounded the trumpet for retreat. Jehanne asked the Bastard to wait a little longer. She mounted her horse and went alone in a vineyard to pray. She finally came back took hold of her standard and went on the parapet of the trench.

As soon as the English saw her, something came over them, for they thought that they had killed her. While she had been away praying, we had time to rest and found food to eat. As Jehanne had her standard in her hand, a soldier came along and grabbed it. There was a sort of tug-of-war between them both for the standard. When the soldier finally got the standard, he rushed forward to the walls. Jehanne cried out, *"My standard, my standard."* When the soldier who had the standard reached the walls, the soldiers who had been resting, saw this, and they got up and became more courageous and charged assaulting the English again, this time getting over the walls; and breaking down the English defence. As the English ran away, they came to the wooden bridge that had been damaged earlier (the drawbridge). A boat had been lit and sent under the bridge. There was a great fire The English soldiers ran across to escape. Many of them including Glasdale fell fully armed in the water below.

Many citizens came out of the Orléans gate and went across the bridge with its 19 arches. They repaired the gaps that were in the bridge, and began to attack the rear of the Tourelles. It became too much for the English when the Tourelles went up in flames. The English abandoned the siege the next day and took the rest of the troops to Meung-Sur-Loire, and other positions along the river. On the evening of the 7th May, we came across the main bridge and entered Orléans. The whole town was celebrating the victory. The bells rang out, and the narrow streets were packed with people dancing and singing. There were many people in the Boucher's house. They congratulated Jehanne and her team for driving the English away.

6.

The Battle for Jargeau, Meung, Beaugency & Patay

When Jehanne had been examined by the Theologians at Poitiers, they asked her for a sign. She said to them, "Take me to Orléans, and you will see the sign." I was proud of her. She did what she said she would do. But there was still more battles to be fought.

After all the celebrations and rejoicing in Orléans, some of the captains, Jehanne and myself left for Blois. At Blois, I said, "So long," and rode up to Tours. Jehanne, later went to Loches to talk with the Dauphin. I hadn't seen Jehanne again until we met at Selles-en-Berry. There, we all gathered in preparation to depart to Jargeau. Jehanne told me that she had spoken to the Dauphin. She wanted him to go to Riems to be crowned – to be anointed just like Clovis, the first king of the Franks, with sacred oil. The court council had plans for moving into Normandy. Even La Hire became a bit angry with the Dauphin for hesitating. Jehanne's plans seemed more credible, because when the king should get himself crowned he will be honored more by the people, and his enemies and their power, would just fade away. After sometime, the Dauphin decided to agree with the plan of Jehanne. It was a dangerous plan; they had first to get rid of the enemies that were in the area.

We arrived at Jargeau, and Jehanne went straight into the attack. Suffolk was the commander in charge there; and he held the bridge; it was the only bridge to get from Orléans to

Gien. Jargeau was a small town with very strong fortified walls, and the fosse was filled with water. Jehanne had with her the Duke d'Alencon, with captains Jean d'Orléans (the bastard of Orléans), Gilles de Rais, Jean Poton de Xaintrailles, and La Hire; and the men of her household. Our force totalled about 1200 men.

The battle started with our forces making a direct assault on the suburbs. We started falling back as the English left the city walls. Jehanne with her standard, rallied us on. She took a scaling ladder to mount the wall. She was hit by a stone that fell on her helmet and knocking her banner away, and she to the ground. Immediately she was up and shouting, "Friends, friends, forward, onwards, our Lord has condemned the English. The day is ours, keep a good heart."

We stayed in the suburbs for the night. The next morning Jehanne called for the English to surrender. They refused. We started bombarding with artillery fire with the small cannons. One of the town's tower fell. We made a breach in the wall, and now it was time to enter with swords. Duke d'Alencon hesitated, and Jehanne urged him on, bringing him to the fact that she had promised his wife to bring him back safely – for he was not married very long. "Are you afraid, gentle duke?" she said. "Do not be afraid, you will be safe."

We stormed the town and Suffolk retreated to the bridge. Many of the garrison were slain in the narrow streets. Suffolk entered into a surrender deal with La Hire which angered the rest of the captains.

Talbot was at Beaugency, and Scales held Meung. We captured all three towns for they had control over important bridge crossing on the Loire. After the English defeat, they made a deal so that they could go away to Paris. Both them and us didn't know that an army had left Paris southwardly, to support the English garrisons in the Loire. Later, we found out. We sent out cavalry scouts to try and seek out the approaching army. The English forces had a thing that they did – it was taught to them by Henry V. They would dismount from their horses to fight on foot; each crossbow-man would drive his sharp stake in front of him; slanting towards the enemy; in order to stop a cavalry charge. It worked most of the time. We, the French, enjoyed riding fast and furious into the enemy. The English crossbow-men usually pick us off easily. Suddenly, the dismounted horsemen would be ready to go into attack with their swords. This strategy always worked for the English and the Scots against ourselves. Jehanne knew about this strategy, so did the bastard, the duke d'Alencon, and La Hire and many more of the captains.

Arthur de Richemont joined us in the evening at Beaugency. He came with about 1,000 horses. Scarred in the face from the battle at Agincourt, Richemont was taken prisoner and carried away to England. After his release he went on the side of the English and Burgundians. He was born around 1393 to Jean IV Duc de Bretagne and Jeanne de Navarre. He was just a bit taller than Jehanne. His mother later became the second wife of the king of England, Henry V. Richemont married Margaret of Burgundy, sister of Phillipe the Good, Duke of Burgundy. Maragaret was the widow of the French Dauphin Louis de Guyenne, a close friend of Richemont. Richemont had problems with the Duke of Bedford who did not give him no command over the forces. Yolande of Aragon grabbed her chance as soon as Richemont left the English and Burgundian side. He was made Constable of France by Charles VII. At the French court there were problems too. Richemont and La Tremoille did not get on. Richemont could not get close to Charles after Richemont's brother Jean V took the side of the

English. Richemont knew he had to get rid of La Tremoille, no matter what. He caused a rebellion to take place, and Charles had it in his mind that Richemont was out to get at him. Charles stopped the rebellion. Later, he offered his pardon and Richemont accepted it. The Constable then went away from the court. The Constable arrival at Beaugency came at a good time; more troops added; and they were good fighting men.

When Jehanne heard of his coming, at first, Duke d'Alencon didn't want to have anything to do with Richemont. Jehanne persuaded him not to leave, so we all rode out to meet Richemont. When we got where the Constable was with his men, both he and Jehanne dismounted. Jehanne moved towards the Constable, knelt down and held his knee. She said to him: "Ah! good Constable, it is not from my doing that you are here, but since you are here, you're very welcome."

"Thank you Jehanne," the Constable said. "I'm sure that together we can do well."

"You're a great soldier," Jehanne replied, "come and meet some of the others."

"You have done well by defeating the English at Orléans," the Constable said as they moved to meet us.

"It was with the help of the King of Heaven that we were able to defeat the English," Jehanne told him.

"I missed out. I would have found it very interesting to be there and whipping the English. Anyway, there are still battles ahead of us."

They reached us and we all rode back to the camp.

When the surrender of Beaugency was accomplished, we moved northwards hoping to come in contact with the new English force. We divided ourselves into three parts; the vanguard; with about 1500 knights and men-at arms; under the command of Poton de Xaintrailles, Ambroise de Loire, and

Etienne de Vignolles (La Hire). Jehanne, being the nominal commander of our army, was in the rear guard – she didn't like to be in that position. There was also the main party. Our scouts were looking around the area close to the town of Patay. Nearing the town of Lignerolles, La Hire and Xaintrailles stopped for a rest; they had sent out scouts on foot to look for the enemy.

In a ravine, Sir John Talbot, the English commander had in position 500 archers. A few hundred metres to the northeast, just behind one of many ridges, the English vanguard stopped. The commander was Sir John Fastolf. He told his 3,000 strong infantry and some cavalry, to rest.

Our scouts came close to where the longbow-men were, they saw no sign of the English. Our scouts continued their search; one of them frightened a deer from where it was, near the English. When the English saw the deer, they let out a hunting cry. Our scouts, on hearing the noise, went back quickly to their temporary camp. It was about 1 o'clock when they came back. They ran to Xaintrailles and La Hire, and told them the location of the English rearguard. The order was given to our horsemen to mount. Within minutes they were on the move.

The English must have seen our scouts and so they started preparing themselves for battle. One of the English tactics was to set sharpened stakes into the ground, facing the enemy. This had the advantage of slowing down the enemy's charge and disrupting it. The English had not yet set up their stakes, and while they were setting up their battle line, our cavalry came over a nearby ridge. We launched a frontal assault and two flanking attacks on the isolated archers. Without their defensive stakes in place – and without any infantry men to support them – the English bowmen were helpless. Most of them died. It was more like a slaughter than a battle. We then headed out for the troops under Fastolf. We were now in a killing mood, nothing was there to stop us. The English had more troops than we had, it took half an hour before the English were routed, and some retreated back on the Old Roman Road to Paris. After about two hours of fighting the battle of Patay was ended. The English had 300 killed and 2,000 captured. We had a mere 100 killed. Talbot was captured; Falstolf escaped.

7.

A Bit of Scottish History

After the strenuous battle at Patay, We headed back to Orléans. There, while waiting for Dauphin to call us, I told Jehanne and some of the captains how Scotland had struggled for its freedom.

We returned to Orléans and waited for the Dauphin to give his permission for us to come to the court at Gien. Before we left Orléans, I told Jehanne and some of the captains about how Scotland had struggled for its freedom from England. I told her also about the *Maid of Norway*. I said: "Scotland had to fight for its freedom from England. It was Robert the Bruce who fought courageously with his men to give Scotland the freedom. In ancient days, England and Scotland had always been in conflict over lands. The English king wanted to be ruler over the Scottish king. Edward I took the throne of England in the year 1272 to 1307. He was a wise and brave king. In the year 1286 Alexander III of Scotland fell over a cliff and died. He had two sons who died before him. He had a daughter, the Queen of Norway who also died. Scotland had no ruler but the young Princess Margaret. Her father was the king of the land in Scotland called *Noroway owre the faem*. Edward decided that he must act to get Scotland to be part of his kingdom; and also for the future rulers. He arranged a marriage between the little Queen and his son Edward, Prince of Wales, who at the time was only 14 years old. A big ship was sent for her, but she did not come back on that ship. Later, a Norwegian ship took her to Scotland to be its Queen. Just as the ship was nearing the land, the little Maid got sick and died..."

"Wait," Jehanne said, "the tears are coming. Jean, this is a sad story but rather interesting. Let me catch my breath, then you can carry on." After a few seconds, she said that she was okay, and ready to hear the rest.

I continued: "Eric II King of Norway was the father of the Maid. Her mother was Margaret, daughter of Alexander III, House of Canmore. She was born 9th April 1283, Tonsberg, Norway. She ascended the throne of Scotland on March 19th 1286 when she was just only two years and some. She didn't get crowned and didn't marry—"

"Come on, Jean," Jehanne broke in, "she was just only a baby!"

"I know that. But in those times, the kings and queens, lords and barons and all those court personnel were busy marrying off their children to get more land and prestige."

"Carry on with your story of Scotland," Jehanne told me.

"After the Maid died," I carried on, "John Balliol took over. There were many people claiming the throne of Scotland – at least 13 in all. The two strongest were John Balliol and Robert Bruce, grandfather of Robert the Bruce, both were descendants of William the Lion, grandfather of the late king. Balliol was the great-grandson of David, Earl of Huttingdon, younger brother of William the Lion; Bruce was the grandson of the same man. Did you get all that?"

"Ah! it's interesting, Jean. The history of Scotland is in some way coupled with that of France. They both had to fight for their freedom," Jehanne said, waiting to hear more.

"Balliol," I told her, "was descended from Earl David's eldest daughter; and Bruce came from a younger one. Edward I invited all the claimants to the Scottish throne to come to

Norham, a castle past which the 'Silver Tweed' runs between wooded banks, dividing England and Scotland. There, he would decide who the right man was to reign over them. The meeting took place on 10th May 1291. This is the year that the real struggle for the right of Scotland started. Edward I picked John Balliol to be the king of Scotland. It was this Balliol who later joined with France against England. He invaded the counties of Norththumberland and Cumberland. Edward I got a fleet of ships, and an army of 30,000 foot soldiers, and 50,000 horsemen. He besieged Berwick -on-Tweed by land and by sea. Berwick at that time was the greatest seaport in Scotland. The garrison there would not give in. They just kept on singing songs. Eventually, the stockade was stormed with one knight losing his life; eight thousand of the citizens were slain. Flemish merchant had locked themselves away in the town hall refusing to surrender. They were all burned alive inside.

"Edward was a horrible king to burn all those people alive," Jehanne said. "He could have shown some pity on them."

"Remember when the Tourelles went up in flames? We never showed any pity whatsoever. And when William Glasdale and his soldiers fell into the freezing water below, fully armed, we could not save them."

"I did shed some tears for them," Jehanne told me.

"It all has to do with war, and war is cruel as everyone knows. Anyway, I will continue with the Scottish history. I shall skip quite a lot, and only explain the main points or else we would be here forever. After the storming of the stockade at Berwick-on-Tweed, later the Scots retaliated by setting fire to the schools that were located at Corbridge and Northumberland and burned to death 200 'little clerks' who were schoolboys."

Jehanne didn't like this part that I had just told to her. But she still wanted to hear the rest and braced herself for more horrible events.

"Edward I," I said to her, "travelled through Scotland as a glorious king. Balliol gave in to Edward all his rights to the kingdom of Scotland. Balliol was imprisoned for three years in London, then he was allowed to go to France where his estates were. He died 13 years later.

Scotland again found itself without a king. Everything were now in the hands of the English governors who took from the Scots whatsoever they wanted. English soldiers went round robbing, beating, and killing the Scots, their wives, their daughters, and their little ones. Edward was in his glory, there came a man whose name was William Wallace, remember that I had mentioned him when the Scottish soldiers came to see you? Well, if it wasn't for Wallace, Scotland would have lost its freedom forever.

Wallace won a great victory over the English at Stirling Bridge in 1297, and then proclaimed himself *Guardian of Scotland*. Edward finally defeated Wallace at Falkirk. Wallace then went underground but was later captured and tried. Then came Robert the Bruce who took over the title of Guardian of Scotland in 1298. After killing his rival, John Comyn, Robert the Bruce claimed the throne. In 1306 he was crowned King of Scone as Robert I. In 1307 he started his campaign to get rid of the English out of Scotland. The difference between you, Jehanne, and Robert the Bruce was that he became king. But you came to drive the English away, and to crown a Dauphin."

"So there is a great strong tie between Scotland and France?"

"Yes," I said. "They've always helped each other and up till now."

"That Bruce, Robert, I mean, was a real warrior from what you have told me."

"He too, at some time had to go underground so that he could get away from his enemies," I told her. "They even used his own dog to track him down. He was just too good for them. In 1328 the Treaty of Edinburgh was signed between between King Robert I and Edward III which recognised Scotland's independence. Scotland had to dig in deep, lots of blood had been spilt, many people wept, unbearable pain suffered, to get the freedom that they so badly needed."

8.

The Coronation of the Dauphin

Now Jehanne is busy preparing for her Loire campaign, to clear the enemy out of the path to Riems. After the coronation, the captains urged her to take Paris.

The Messenger came with great news. We can now leave Orléans and head to Gien.

When we got there, Jehanne sent out news about her Loire campaign. We captured the towns of Crevant, Auxerre, Saint-Florenten, Brinon and Saint-Phal, they all accepted Charles as their king. Troyes was a bit difficult, there were Burgundian soldiers in it. They failed to open up their gates and hand over the keys to the king. They didn't trust Jehanne because she had said that she was sent from God. They had a preacher among them who was called Brother Richard. They sent him out to see if Jehanne was really who she said she was. Jehanne had already sent letters out; to Philip the Good, the Duke of Burgundy. She wanted him to give up the English cause and return being friends once again, with France. The people of Troyes had also received letters from her. The Friar, Brother Richard saw nothing bad about Jehanne, and he stayed with her. Jehanne got her forces ready to attack but the citizens surrendered. Jehanne rode through the gates of Troyes with the Dauphin, the nobles, the captains and the men-at-arms. Jehanne had also tried to get the Dauphin to accept the Constable at the coronation but he refused.

From Troyes, we moved to Chalons. At that time, many

people were attaching themselves to the party of the Dauphin Chalons surrendered and so we moved to Sepsaults; a place not very far from Riems.

The Dauphin still was hesitating, he had not made up his mind completely of what he wanted to do. I saw how Jehanne acted, and I knew that she was not going to give in now that she had gotten him this far. She convinced him to continue his journey to Riems On Saturday 16th July officials from Riems met with the Dauphin and his party and accepted him as king. That evening, preparations were hurriedly made for the coronation.

On the 17th July 1429 at about 09.00 am, the king entered the cathedral to be crowned. It was a fair day and there were many people out – more of them to see Jehanne – than the king.

Riems cathedral was known as the cathedral of Notre-Dame. It was very large, and had room to take in many people. It was first erected in 1211 but was later damaged during World War 1. The ceremony of the anointing took place just like that when Clovis and all the French kings got anointed – with the sacred oil. When the crown was set on the Dauphin's head, suddenly, there were lots of shouting from the soldiers and the people. I noticed tears were in Jehanne's eyes and she stood there close to the altar, and close to the king, still hanging on to her Standard. She knelt down, took hold of the king's knee and said," Noble king, now is God's will accomplished. You, and you alone, noble king, is the true king. The kingdom of France is rightly yours. I have done the two things that the King of Heaven commanded me to do – lift the siege – and get you to this city of Riems for your anointing." Now the Dauphin was King Charles VII.

On the 29th July Jehanne mobilizes her troops at Chateau-Theiry. Two days later Charles declared that the citizens of

Domremy and Greux are exempt from taxation. In the first week of the month of August, the Duke of Bedford and the Duke of Burgundy declares Charles's kingship and anointing as invalid. In the same month, we had skirmishes with the English forces at Montpilloy. Coming to the end of the month, Charles signed a four months truce with the Duke of Burgundy. Jehanne knew nothing about it. No sooner was the coronation done with, most of the captains and men-at-arms were talking about Paris. They all agreed that that was the next step to take; and were eager to attack right away. Jehanne herself had no intention of attacking Paris but went along with the rest of the captains. Her voices hadn't given her permission to make an attack. After many long debates, the king gave the order to make the move.

D'Alencon and Jehanne left in the vanguard. When we got to St. Denis, we settled in a place called La Chapelle. The king delayed his coming so that d'Alencon had to go personally to fetch him. When he finally arrived it was 7th September.

Paris was quite old. The Gauls settled there around 250 BC. It had the name of Lutetia in olden times. It came into the hands of the Romans around 52 BC. In front of the gate Porte Saint-Honore, was a moat filled with water. The walls were very high and the place was very well fortified.

On the morning of 8th September 1429, Jehanne, myself, Duke d'Alencon, Gilles de Rais, Jean de Brosse Boussac, and La Hire left La Chapelle and went to the Porte Saint-Honore. There were about 2,000 English plus the population defending Paris. In this type of warfare, tactics are often used, like getting the citizens to turn against the soldiers occupying them, and open the gates. Jehanne was very good at that. She would always shout up at them and mentioning the King of Heaven, and what would happen if they didn't surrender. Paris was commanded by Simon Morhier and Governor Jean de Villiers de L'Isle-Adam.

Jehanne started placing the artillery in position, she was very good at that; then she crossed the moat with the intention of getting to the Porte Saint-Honore gate. It was strongly defended. On the edge of the moat she told the citizens and the soldiers to give up quickly, Jesus sake, for if they did not do so before the night fall, she and her soldiers would enter by force whether they like it or not;and they would all be put to death without mercy. With the pole of her banner she tested to see how deep the moat was, then she called out for faggots. It was about Midday when the attack on Paris started.

The assault was very fierce and cruel. There were lots of arrows flying all over the place and the cannon balls from the English were too much for us. Jehanne got hit in the thigh with a crossbow, just before evening and was taken back to her tent. The standard bearer got hit as well. Jehanne wanted us to continue fighting for we were not far off from taking Paris. We retreated.

The following day, Jehanne told d'Alencon to get the soldiers ready to start the attack again . Just then, a message came from the king that we must not continue. There was a bridge that d'Alencon and his men had rigged up across the river, but it was taken down in the night by orders of the king. Jehanne gave her suit of armour as an offering on the altar at Saint Denis. She had to say goodbye to some of her brave soldiers who were going away to Normandy to fight. Duke d'Alencon went as well after the army was disbanded. He wanted to take Jehanne with him, but those who were in charge of the war-council did not allow it. They were Sire de Gaucourt, Georges de la Tremoille, and Regnalt de Chartres. Jehanne was told to rest and let the wound that she got at Paris, heal. She stayed at Bourges.

9.

The Capture of Jehanne

Simple mistakes can cause the loss of many lives. From what I have seen Jehanne was a great soldier and comrade. Everyone liked her. There was a bit of stubbornness in her. Rarely, did she fail to deliver. The way she was taken was through intrigue.

When the army was finally disbanded, I had not yet made up my mind what I wanted to do. Should I stay with Jehanne or back to Tours? I had been a long time away from my family; and I missed them very much. Jehanne was left at this time with only a small group, a few hardened veterans. She hadn't the support that she always had when the Royal army was around. Still, she did not give in, but was more determined to continue. From childhood I knew Jehanne, I knew what she was like; she had that stubborn streak; but was very kind; always working very hard. She loved horses very much. She could tell if a horse was fit for war or not. In fact, she told me one time that she got into trouble by telling a bishop that the horse he had given her weren't a real horse. She commanded her soldiers well, she had a good sense of humor. She was just a little shorter than myself, about five foot five inches tall. Her hair back at Domremy was long. She told me that when she went to Vaucouleurs, and was accepted to go to Chinon, she had it cut, short and round. On the right of her neck, she had a little red mark. Her eyes were rather penetrating, a brownish color. I felt at times that she was two person in one. Very protective and sensitive. Tears come very quickly, and she like to be alone and relaxing. Most of all, she love to go to mass or hear it sung. There's no doubt about it that she was extremely religious. It was from all this that I made up my mind and said to myself that I would stay with her to the end.

George de la Tremoille had trouble with a mercenary who was causing trouble at a place called Saint-Pierre-le Moutier. He called Jehanne and gave her orders to go after this mercenary. Saint-Pierre-le Moutier was a small town heavily guarded and fortified. It had a very deep moat. We besieged the town. The siege was rather difficult. It was under the command of d'Albret accompanied by Marshall Boussac and the Count of Montpensier. We had to retreat. While we were there, Jean d'Aulon, the squire of Jehanne, saw us with only about three other soldiers. He had been injured. He rode up and asked her what she was doing here alone, and why she did not retreat like all the others. She removed her sallet (a flat top helmet) from her head and answered that she wasn't alone; and that she still had in her company fifty thousand men; and that she would not depart from there until she had taken the city. I chuckled for a while, but didn't let her see me do so. There were only about five of us with Jehanne included. D'Aulon said to her directly that she should leave and retire as the others had done; but she told him to bring some bundles of sticks and wicker hurdles to make a bridge over the town's moat so that they could approach better. She cried out in a loud voice: "To the bundles and hurdles, everybody, make the bridge!" – which was prepared swiftly, and then accomplished. I saw how amazed D'Aulon was when the city was taken all at once by her assault without finding much resistance.

On the 16th November 1429 King Henry VI was crowned at Westminister. It was at this time the Duke of Bedford had trouble recruiting men for France, "through the fear of the devices of the Maid." A letter was given to Jehanne from Charles declaring nobility on her family and herself. In January 1430 we are at a banquet in Orléans. Things had not been going well for Jehanne after the failure to take Paris and La Charite-sur-Loire. Philip the Good was now planning to take over Champagne and Brie. Jehanne promised she would defend those areas. There were many marauding gangs around, groups of mercenaries, with their leaders taking over small towns. George de la Tremoille had sent Jehanne against one of those groups, whose leader had been his worst enemy. We had no problem whatsoever in defeating this mercenary leader. At this time, La Tremoille and the Archbishop had control over the court, and going against many good decisions that Jehanne had made. They were involved in trying to make some kind of truce with Philip the Good which Jehanne knew would not come about. Charles VII, King of France had been duped many times by the English and the Burgundians. At one time Jehanne got so fed up with Charles and the court, that she left and went out in the field for two weeks; all because Charles could not make a decision, he kept on hesitating.

The court was now at Sully; it got so bad this time that Jehanne left the court for good without telling anyone. She left with her brothers, myself, a few servants and only a few soldiers. We went to Melun. Her voices had told her that she would be taken prisoner before the feast of St. John. We didn't stay in Melun very long, we left and went to Lagny, passing through areas filled with enemies and bands of Burgundians pillaging, robbing churches and villages; destroying fields wherever they happen to pass. This band of Burgundians were led by Franquet d'Arras. We went after them. Our group totalled about 400, along with some noblemen. We had a Scots whose name was

Hugh Kennedy We attacked the group, Franquet and his men fought ferociously but failed to come out on top. Franquet was captured and taken as prisoner; he was brought back to Lagny to be ransomed. The law found him to be a murderer, a robber, and the poor didn't mean anything to him, he was tried, found guilty and was beheaded.

Inside a church in Lagny there was a child whom the parents said was dead. There were some maidens praying for the baby, Jehanne joined them. The eyes of the child were opened, it yawned, a few times, was baptized and then it died. We visited other places where there was much danger. We went to Compiegne while the Archbishop was a part of the group. On one of our visit to Compiegne, Jehanne went to an early mass in the church of St. Jacques. When the service had ended, she told some people and many children that she had been sold and betrayed, and that she will soon die. Later, we got news that Compiegne was in trouble. It was the HQ of Charles and the people had received him as their king. Plans were being made by the Burgundians to take back Compiegne. We left Compiegne and visited many other places.

We are at Crepy-en-Valois when we heard news that the Duke of Burgundy was planning to take over Compiegne.

"We shall all go," Jehanne said, "and help our dear friends. We musn't let them think that we have abandoned them We shall ride hard and fast and get there before dawn."

I said to Jehanne, "Do you think we have enough troops for this Compiegne affair?"

She said, "By my staff, we're enough! I shall go and see my good friends there."

It was 22nd May 1430, getting close to midnight. We all set out riding through the dark forest. We rode fast and got to Compiegne in good time. We were really tired, and went straight away to rest. Around five in the evening, Jehanne decided to go and do a recce.

The Burgundians had a camp at Margny with another one at Clairoix; the English had their HQ at Venette. Compiegne had a boulevard at the end of its drawbridge. Jehanne then decide to attack Margny, and then take on Clairoix; and then be ready for the Duke of Burgundy and his forces. She totally forgot about the English. Before she left Compiegne, she had already made plans with governor Flavy, to make sure that the boulevard was defended; and boats placed ready in case of a retreat. The attack on Margny went off very well, they gave in. The camp at Clairoix had sent troops to aid Margny, but they were driven back. Attacking and retreating between the Burgundians and ourselves went on for some time – then the English joined in.

There was a great panic in our ranks as we started retreating. Some went to where the boats were, others to the boulevard trying to cross the drawbridge. The archers stationed there did absolutely nothing, fearing they might kill their own people – so close the English were. Jehanne was at the front making a direct assault, not knowing what was taking place at the drawbridge. She kept on shouting, "Forward, they are ours!"

At that moment, we came to our senses, and saw what was really happening. We tried to get Jehanne to retreat, she was really in the thick of the fighting. We managed to circle around her to make it harder for the enemy to get at her. We got to the barrier of the boulevard and I went through on my horse along with some crowds and other soldiers. Jehanne should have been just behind us but it was not so. Flavy had closed the barrier to the boulevard, and the drawbridge was taken up; and the gates being closed. The crowds that had followed to fight the enemy, were now pushing and trampling down on each other in an effort to get through the barrier and through the boulevard. The English lances were not far behind them. And that must have been the reason why Flavy took the drawbridge up. The soldiers with Jehanne scattered, trying to get to another gate. In that moment, Jehanne was pulled off her horse by her cape that was flowing behind her. I didn't see this happen, I was told about it later.

From where I was on my horse, I couldn't see anything but the closed gates blocking my view, and the crowds of citizens who had already rushed in, and all around me. I turned my horse round a few times and cursing vehemently for what had taken place. Jehanne should have been here with me, safe, and out of reach of the English and the Burgundians. The one thing she had feared had now come to pass – to be captured by the Burgundians. I was thinking now it's better the Burgundians. God knows what those English men would have done, if she had fallen into their hands. She was taken captive by a Burgundian soldier, the bastard of Wandome, one of John of Luxembourg's men. Knowing Jehanne, she would not have surrendered easily, she would have made it hard for them. She was one hell of a woman, they don't come like her often. She was one of those rare ones. I turned by horse forward, sore at heart, and grieving for my childhood friend – Jehanne.

The End.